# Monty's
# Ups and Downs

## Colin West

Collins

**Look out for more *Jets* from Collins**

*Jessy Runs Away* • *Best Friends* • **Rachel Anderson**

*Ivana the Inventor* • *Ernest the Heroic Lion Tamer* • **Damon Burnard**

*Two Hoots* • *Almost Goodbye Guzzler* • **Helen Cresswell**

*Shadows on the Barn* • **Sarah Garland**

*Nora Bone* • *The Mystery of Lydia Dustbin's Diamonds* • **Brough Girling**

*Thing on Two Legs* • *Thing in a Box* • **Diana Hendry**

*Desperate for a Dog* • *More Dog Trouble* • **Rose Impey**

*Georgie and the Dragon* • *Georgie and the Planet Raider* • **Julia Jarman**

*Cowardy Cowardy Cutlass* • *Free With Every Pack* • **Robin Kingsland**

*Mossop's Last Chance* • *Mum's the Word* • **Michael Morpurgo**

*Hiccup Harry* • *Harry Moves House* • **Chris Powling**

*Rattle and Hum, Robot Detectives* • **Frank Rodgers**

*Our Toilet's Haunted* • **John Talbot**

*Rhyming Russell* • *Messages* • **Pat Thomson**

*Monty the Dog Who Wears Glasses* • *Monty Ahoy* • *Monty Bites Back* • *Monty Must Be Magic* • *Monty Up to his Neck in Trouble* • *Monty's Ups and Downs* • **Colin West**

*Ging Gang Goolie, it's an Alien* • *Stone the Crows, it's a Vacuum Cleaner* • **Bob Wilson**

First published by A & C Black Ltd in 1996
Published by Collins in 1997
10 9 8 7 6 5 4
Collins is an imprint of HarperCollins*Publishers* Ltd,
77–85 Fulham Palace Road, Hammersmith, London W6 8JB

ISBN 0 00 675207 1

Text and illustrations © Colin West 1996

Colin West asserts the moral right to
be identified as the author/illustrator of the work.
A CIP record for this title is available from the British Library.
Printed and bound in Great Britain by Clays Ltd, St Ives plc

# Monty and the Raffle

Simon and Josie Sprod's school was
holding a Bumper Bazaar. There
were stalls selling tinned food,
house plants, knitted items and lots
more besides . . .

...Such as scrumptious home-made cakes!

Josie and Simon were running the raffle stall. The third prize was a box of chocolates.

The second prize was a tin of fancy biscuits ...

... and the first prize was a teddy bear in a funny hat.

Who'd ever want to win first prize?

Monty, the dog who wears glasses, wasn't really supposed to be at school. So Simon and Josie told him to stay hidden under the table.

The bazaar was busy, but no one was buying raffle tickets. Josie and Simon needed to make the first prize look more exciting.

They borrowed Monty's glasses and perched them on the teddy's nose.

Monty's glasses did the trick!
Lots of people noticed the teddy and
came to buy raffle tickets.

Even Mrs Prendlethorpe, the
Headmistress was impressed.

But Monty was fed up. He missed his glasses and he was getting peckish. The cakes on the next stall looked very tempting.

But as Monty slyly stretched over
the table, disaster struck!

He knocked the teddy bear off its
stand and it fell head first into a big
chocolate cake!

SQUELCH!

'Oh no, Monty, look what you've done!' wailed Simon.
There was worse to come.
Josie noticed Mrs Prendlethorpe making her way towards them.

But the teddy was in a dreadful state. Then Josie had a brainwave. She grabbed Monty, put his glasses back on, and added the funny hat.

Then Josie sat Monty on the table and told him not to move a muscle. 'Mrs P might not notice if you keep quite still,' she whispered.

Josie held her breath as the Head Teacher approached. 'It's time for me to make the prize draw,' she told them.

With that, Mrs Prendlethorpe
picked up Monty.

Josie and Simon followed with the
other prizes.

But as they
reached the
stage,
Monty had
another
mishap.

He needed to scratch his nose, but
dared not move. He twitched his
nose a bit and the itch got worse.
Suddenly, he felt a sneeze coming
on . . .

Achoo!

Mrs Prendlethorpe had the shock of her life! She dropped Monty and ran out of the hall screaming.

Simon and Josie had to make the draw for the raffle themselves. (But not before Monty had helped lick the teddy bear clean!)

# Monty and the Antique Vase

It was the summer holidays and the Sprod family were looking forward to a visit from Granny.

Mrs Sprod had a quiet word with her husband.

We'll have to search out that old vase your mother gave us last Christmas

Mr Sprod's face dropped. He *hated* the ugly vase Granny had given them. He felt sure she'd picked it up at a Car Boot Sale.

But whenever Granny visited, they had to display the vase to be polite. So Mr Sprod unearthed it from the cupboard and blew off the cobwebs.

'I wish we didn't have to do this every time Granny comes,' thought Mr Sprod. But then he had a naughty idea.

Monty's rather clumsy. Maybe he could 'accidentally' break it!

Mr Sprod placed the vase on the spindly table in the hall. Then he banged on the biscuit tin and called Monty.

Monty raced in from the garden and pelted down the hallway.

The table wobbled as Monty
bounded past . . .

. . . the
vase
       t
        u m
           b
             l
              e
               d
                 o
                   f
                    f . . .

. . . and smashed on the floor.

CRASH!

Monty stopped in his tracks.

He dreaded what Mr Sprod might
do. But Mr Sprod was actually
smiling. He bent down and
whispered in Monty's ear.

Monty was very confused, but he munched on the biscuit all the same.

Never look a gift horse in the mouth!

Mr Sprod swept up the broken vase and was in a happy mood all afternoon.

Whistle while you work ♪♪♪

That evening, Mr Sprod settled down
to watch his favourite TV show,
*Antiques on the Road*. Suddenly he
could hardly believe his eyes.

There on the screen was a vase, just
like Granny's. Then he could hardly
believe his ears.

This is a very charming vase and it's worth about £1,000!

Eric Knowall

Mr Sprod leapt up and started
tearing out his hair.
He was hopping mad!

# Monty's Football Match

Simon, Josie and Granny Sprod
were at the park with Monty. Simon
noticed some friends kicking a ball
around.

Andrew invited the Sprods to a
game of football.

Andrew, Alice
and Adam
The 'A' Team

V.

Simon, Josie
and Granny
The Sprod
Superstars

They marked out one goal using
their bags.

Then they went to mark out the other goal. They used Granny's big handbag for one post and looked round for something for the other.

'I know!' said Alice, snapping her fingers.

Monty looked startled. He didn't fancy being a goal post.

But Alice *was* serious, and so reluctantly the Sprods agreed.

They sat Monty down firmly and
Granny stood in goal at the opposite
end. Then they kicked off and the
'A' team showed off their skills.

Adam was good at passing.

Alice was good at heading.

And Andrew was good at dribbling.

The Sprod Superstars weren't as good. Granny wasn't the best goalie in the world. And Simon and Josie couldn't kick straight.

The score was soon Three-Nil to the 'A' team.

Then Monty had a winning idea.

When no one was looking, he slowly edged away from his other goal post.

Sure enough, next time Simon tried
to score, the ball went in the goal!

Soon Josie headed in another.
(Although Monty had to use his
head a bit, too!)

Then Granny scored with a
dramatic drop kick. It was now
Three-All!

The 'A' team were worried about
the way the game was going.
'Let's change ends,' they declared.

As they did so, Monty reversed his
plan. This time he edged *nearer*
Granny's handbag.

Adam, Andrew and Alice had real trouble trying to get one past Granny.

In the second half, the 'A' team didn't score once. But a lucky shot from Simon brought the final score to Four-Three!

# Monty's Midnight Snack

It was midnight and everyone in the
Sprod household was fast asleep.

Everyone that is, except Monty,
who was still wide awake.

Although Monty had eaten three square meals during the day, he was still thinking of food.

Monty crept over to the fridge. It was dark in the kitchen but he could just make out the shape of the fridge door handle.

Monty stretched as high as he could.

Then Monty had an idea.

Monty nudged his basket on to its
side and tipped it upside-down.

He pushed it towards the fridge and
hopped on.

Now Monty could reach the handle, and he slowly pulled the door open.

The light from inside the fridge lit up the dark room. Monty was dazzled by the goodies inside.

Of all the things,
Monty particularly
fancied a bowl of
trifle which was on
the top shelf.

Monty stretched himself, but he
couldn't quite reach it.

Monty stuck out his tongue as far as it would go. He went up on tip-toe. But he seemed to be getting no nearer the bowl of trifle.

Then Monty noticed the reason why – the basket was slowly slipping away from under his feet.

Suddenly the basket wasn't there at all. Monty tried to grab hold of something. He reached out . . . and knocked the trifle off its shelf.

Monty fell to the floor. So did the trifle!

# Monty's Shopping Trip

Simon and Josie were doing some
last-minute Christmas shopping
with Monty.

The children left Monty outside the store.

Monty sat and waited . . . and waited . . . and waited. He was getting colder by the minute.

'Brrr! I bet it's nice and warm inside the store,' he thought.

Monty managed to slip out of his collar.

Monty headed for the entrance of Borridge's. It seemed a *very* strange door indeed.

Monty spun round ten times before he managed to come out the other side.

He felt quite dizzy.
He walked round in a daze looking for Josie and Simon.

Monty's nose was twitching at all sorts of exotic smells. He didn't like them much.

Monty managed to hop inside the lift just before the doors almost chopped him in half.

Someone pushed the button for the
fourth floor and the lift ascended
very suddenly . . .

. . . and then stopped with a jolt.

Monty staggered out and walked a few steps. There were rowing machines and exercise bikes, but still no sign of Simon or Josie.

Monty was feeling really queasy by
now. The revolving door, the exotic
smells and the ride in the lift had
made him feel funny inside.

Monty saw a comfy-looking thing a
bit like a camp-bed and thought
he'd have a lie down.

He jumped up on to the 'camp-bed',
but was soon in for a surprise.

It was *very* springy indeed, and the
more he tried to make himself
comfy, the more he bounced
around.

# A crowd started gathering as . . .

. . . first Monty went up . . . . . . . . and then came down . . . . . . . .

£49.99

Soon Monty

was bouncing

all over

the place.

Luckily before long, a big man
caught Monty in his arms.

Monty's world was spinning around. But as he came back to earth, he heard a familiar voice.

Suddenly the store manager
stepped forward.
'Is this your dog?' he asked Josie
and Simon.

'Well, he's done no real harm I
suppose,' said the manager.

In fact, the manager soon realised Monty had drawn a big crowd to the Sports Department. What's more, everyone wanted to spend their money!

The manager thought the children
deserved a small reward. He picked
up a super looking tennis racket
and presented it to them.

'Perhaps your dog could give a performance every day!' the manager joked as they left. But Monty had had enough ups and downs to last a lifetime!